my heart
is an ant
carrying
the heaviest things
back home

Written and Illustrated by Samantha Heeley

Cover Art by Samantha Heeley

ISBN: 9798456238887

hair

backbone

& other things i grew

a collection of poems and prose

SAMANTHA HEELEY

Dedicated to those who dared to be the dance

of the candle flame on my darkest days

CONTENTS

it's a masquerade
mandatory attendance
an eggshell dance floor

THIS YEAR I'VE BEEN

An over steeped tea bag.
Racoon road kill.
Without teeth. Hungry.

An autopsy. Open chest.
A spine of a book.
Vulnerable. Desperate. Tested.

A beige crayon.
An egg. Deviled.
The kite caught in the tree.
Forgotten.

A pause.

Aphrodite. Forgiveness.
A sunflower field. Wide and wild.
A mood ring stuck on blue.
Broken winged. Mended. A lemon.
Humbled.
Painted black. A snowflake.
Learning bird songs.
A morning. Crested.
Loved.
Still.

CAVALRY

Gone is the courage

of the cavalry. Reality wears
a blindfold of this

repetitive reverie. The one where we
spread our wings and are free

Gone is the grace

of the eagle. We fly now with
the hunger of the vulture. Leaving

reverence in the nest. The wind no longer
carries the song of a sparrow;

but the caw of the crow

KILLDEER

the morning sky is ochre
the horizon, coy
we rose so hungry

we want to eat the eyes of everything
your whisper is a wisp of spider silk
that wakes my spine

you make my back arch in such a way
that it reminds you of Moab
you feel at home

this is the moment we want to stay in forever
we know this as soon as we leave it
we go into hiding

under unfurled monarch wings
we learn to linger in throats of swallows
until they take us south

we find refuge in
the rufous fringe of the Killdeer
learn how to play dead

we've perfected the art of pretending
a broken wing. perhaps. this time
next. a broken heart

FORGIVENESS

I forgive you for being a water sign
that's been more lazy river, more placid lake,
when you have the take of ocean undertow
raging under your skin.

For shrinking, contorting and ignoring warnings
while you try to fit in places not meant for you.
For not speaking up, speaking out, speaking louder.
For relying only on a body language which nobody
understands.

I forgive you for the time in the townhouse
when you burned the eggs so badly they ended
up on the ceiling and the walls and the neighbour
had to call the fire department.

I forgive you for living in *italics*. Your mouth being a **bold**
thing. Your mind is <u>underlined</u> and all too often undermined.
For the line you never draw but are quick to cross.
I forgive you for giving so much of yourself away
that you no longer have a shadow.

I forgive you for being a creature of habit. Of comfort. The
mouse in the house that has escaped the farmer's field and calls
itself a wild thing. For secretly seeking shelter. For being caught
by the clawless cat.

I forgive you for the times you doused the house
in kerosene but your heart wouldn't let your hands
strike the match. For doubting that you could save them.
I forgive you for this new kind of vertigo. For not knowing
which direction you're being pulled when everything is
spinning out of control.

I *(am trying really hard to)* forgive you for your complacency.
Your conformity. What you normally wouldn't fold into if you
weren't so tired. I forgive you for being strong in the only way
you know. I forgive you for momentarily forgetting
exactly who you are.

NIGHT IS A NARCISSIST

Tonight is a cold cathedral
                    gothic

Almost apothecary in the delivery
of giving me what I need

Tonight slides cold steel air down
                          my spine

Raises the skin there
I'm aware of every hair standing

at attention. Tonight smells slightly

of tarragon. Reminds me of thanksgiving
The pleasantries are still stuck

inside like the gizzards

Tonight is nervous and needy
A little too 'look at me'. So I look

a little too long and she fades away
She's always doing that

Tonight mothers a new moon
cutting teeth on corners of clouds

Tonight carries an echo

COAL AND CONSEQUENCE

A couple
A solitaire
A church. A white dress. Crowd. Vows
You;   Taking a wife
Me;   Taking a name
I miss the syllables of who I once was
Before I knew what I wanted
I said wanted another band
Like bookends
Like a heavier finger would prove something
Add some shine to the dull
Maybe to prove that love was still a circle
Round. A new moon. No longer newlyweds. 5 years in
Put it in a wooden box. Call it traditional
Call it unconditional. 10 years in
We're shining like aluminum foil
I don't believe in diamonds anymore, nor mining
Just coal and consequence
The pressure of saying yes will harden anything
We book-marked stars, once
Gave clouds a name
Back then my blood was sugar water
Hummingbirds lived in my chest
The power of a small fast flutter was how I would breath
Before they flew away
Before my body was a river run dry

RELAX
(after Ellen Bass)

Bad things are going to happen.
You will crash your mother's car.
Carry pieces of it in your pocket.
Lose the locket she gave you. The ruby ring.
This is why you cannot have nice things.
You will do the thing they tell you to do.
The white dress.
Nothing more. Nothing less.
You will endure a pain that puts your eyes
in the back of your head.
The nurse tells you there is no time for the epidural.
It's time to push.
You split in half just before you're made whole.
You will not know why your baby is crying.
The baby will not know why you are crying.
You cry together until the baby falls asleep on your breast.
You will call your mother for the recipe.
Burn the good cut of meat.
Wonder how she did it.
Your boss will find a poem you printed at work.
You tell her it's because you were seated in a broom closet.
No windows. You needed an escape.
You quit because she could not understand a metaphor.

You will buy a house that's not right.
Find mice under your mattress. Find grey hair
squirrels nesting in the attic. Breeding.
Find bigots and maggots and other things that feed off of
other living things. Need less cultivation, more culture.
Your spouse will become a stranger. All your conversations will
be inter

rupted. Fall asleep instead of fuck. Your bones are so tired.
He brings you coffee in the morning. This love is 20 years old.
You've sold your house. You're packing. You have two
diplomas you use for wrapping your wedding china.
One day you'll get so angry. Break the butter dish in front of
the children. Tell them it slipped. Tell them a lie about butter -
fingers. Make a silly face. Get lost in the song of their laughter.
You forget the reason you broke it and that you are bleeding
and now you are laughing too.

FLATLINE

I find myself infatuated with this particularly grey day
The last Tuesday in October staying in my bones

A blue moon waits in the balance
Winter is walking on tiptoes

The clouds puff their chests; have egos
How dare they be so boisterous

An afternoon sky lined with insensitivity
A reminder of all impossible things my palms will never hold

I have to admit, I admire the power of anything
that can take my fire and colour me monotone

This metronome of home and gone again
The battle between the blank page and pen

The not knowing of where or when has made
an unsettled sea of uncertainty in my stomach

There is an acoustic playlist playing games with my heart
It is a love song. All I hear is the hollow of the guitar

The dismantling of a tune leaves me with one note
I hum a flatline

RITUALS

Twilight tongues the horizon
A thirsty reach for the celestial sea
Aquarius calls for an obedient open mouth
to pour his water weight into
Eridanus is polluted with old dead fish
The dry-eyed sky blinks
Swallows the day behind her eyelids
Each star is a lie
The sky is full
Place your faith in a lunar illusion
Let the moonlit music box melody play
Darkness dances all night long on the tips of her toes
Pirouettes on the precipice of a new day
This ritual makes for a rigid soleus
The blood pools and dries by morning
The sun rises in shades of red

TWENTY ONE FOR AFTER EIGHT

It's after eight
days melt into nights
silence bends an arm
follows the finger shadow
to the knuckle bone
pointing home

PERMANENT

First set;
A cutting of milk teeth
First taste of temporary things
Exfoliating
Allowing our arches
to become home
to a permanent occlusion
A conclusion
that there is no need to be polite
Let the canines bite
Let the molars chew
on sweet nothings
Until they have to be pulled
from our mandible proving
nothing is permanent

WHEN I CLOSE MY EYES

When I close my eyes
I sink
There is a new moon in my mouth
I am swimming in a fever

There is no shape here
The walls have fallen away
All that is left is a large window
I fall out of

Into a pool
of old blood
Thick with copper acoustics
Silence the smell

I hang in a nebula
The archer's arrow at my temple
A hook finds the corner of my mouth
Cuts the cheek, expands the vestibule

I can feel you
You visit every vertebrae
with a soft breath
You leave before I can invite you in

The curtains sway against the wall
The windows are closed
The skinny black cat is an omen
I wake up in your smile

BLACKEST
(after Bluets by Maggie Nelson)

1. the last time i was pure. cells in a liquid black sac inside of a redheaded woman. multiplying until i was baby enough to escape and call her mother. how i cried all day. craved the bruise of nightfall. the redheaded woman would rock me. it was in the arms of darkness that i could finally fall asleep. back of an eyelid, inside of closed mouth black.

2. dark water. night sky on earth. a satin slip on naked skin. sinking into a sinister silence. a filling of ears. nostrils. not knowing drowning but wanting to.

3. coffee. souls of old men. licorice. dark things I prefer to pull through my teeth. the colour of cavities. magic. ink. bats and ravens. bellies of butterflies. in good company with blue. silhouettes and shadows. anything that will dance against a wall. your hair before the grey quietly crept in. burnt dinners. we ate. we are always hungry. blackout poetry; a temporary cure for writer's block. blackout drunk. my favourite way to forget you. the colour of trying.

4. black tie affairs. the colour a mistress wears well. the shade of confusion. the contusion left on the inside of a right thigh. the most tender part of a neck. love notes that are never meant to stay. after all, you are a hidden piece of scrap paper filled with handwriting that always knows what to say. pupils are a brave place to hide what you never want to be found. your eyes become two black holes. forever is dark. i am swimming.

THE POET AT 37
(after Erika Sánchez/ after Larry Levis)

She comes out at night
A lone wolf; howling
She smokes out a room
Sits in the grey
Dreams of being a cloud
A particularly heavy, dark cloud
She wants to own the lightning
The electricity she feels in her veins

She holds fine wine in her cheek
Robust with a boldness
that comes with getting older
She's dropped out of the rat race
No more running
No more chasing
Embraces the stillness

She is the hanging J of a caterpillar
Pupa. Chrysalis.
In the mess of metamorphosis
Waiting for wings

Prefers cold pressed paper. More tooth
Prefers things with bite
Sharpens her pencil with her teeth
Writes truth on whatever she can find
Tucks it in your pocket

She undresses confidently
Bares herself. Wants the lights on
She knows the power in her hips. Her lips
Yet knows that no one is listening

Yet

She is in her prime and wants to fuck
Fascism. Patriarchy. The system
Sit on the face of misogyny
Snuff them out

Refuses to cut her hair or wear new clothes
The world is so wasteful and boastful
She writes of her lovers
She writes off egocentrics
She's an enigma. An alien
She dreams of life on Mars or a star
or somewhere otherworldly and far, far away

She cuts the sugar from her coffee
Her smile. Her vocabulary
Always talking. Just wanting to be heard
Learning to listen
Trusts only her intuition

Her hands hold a pen
Her mouth opens wide
and nothing comes out

DATE ME
By Samantha Heeley (after Amy Kay)

I dare you. But first,
Tell me your birth date. And time. And the township
in which you exited your mother's middle.
Tell me, have you ever kissed an ocean and are you scared
of drowning?
Tell me, have you ever pressed your ear to the opening of a
conch shell. My heart lives there.
Tell me, *everything.*

I want a mouth that is worldly. Dirty. That has tasted things
known as delicacies. A mouth that knows what it wants.
A mouth that can handle a little bit of bitter and salt.
Hands that can travel my body without a tour guide.

I'll impress you with how fast I can forget your middle name,
yet remember how many times you looked at me a little too
long. How I remember the exact shade of grey that circles your
eyes. How they are the colour of storm clouds.

I dress in caution tape, so don't say I didn't warn you. I'm
honey bee sweet with the sting of starved desert scorpion.
Sometimes I can be a mess and found down on the cold
kitchen tile. I'm the one crying in the greeting card aisle.
The one pulling you onto the dance floor, pulling you closer,
singing karaoke in the taxi cab that's bringing you back to my
place.

I am soft as a kitten's belly. Spontaneous as a summer
hailstorm. Stubborn as an oil stain. Known to stick
to your teeth like tar. I pray to dead poets and have the
patience of a toddler. I ask a lot of questions.
Like why are you here with me and what is this moment
made of. Will there be more of them?

Best compared to putting your hands up when riding
that old wooden roller coaster you're not sure you trust.
A little bit of stomach lurch, a lot of uncertainty,
having so much fun you think '*it's okay if I fall*'

ENIGMA

You've fallen in love with a stranger you've picked up off the bathroom floor. She's a devastating mess but you're a sucker for her smile. You know there is no fostering or fixing her as well as you know your stone cold heart cannot get too close to her fire. You're willing to love her pieces all at once. As close as we will get to being whole. You know this because you've been broken before and are used to loving ghosts. Just not living ones. Maybe you can get used to this. You don't want another haunting but it's too late because she's embedded in your membrane. She is filthy. You tell her to watch her mouth. Watching her mouth is your favourite pastime. The curves of her cursing.

You hate that you love how she never has a plan. How she's serial with her spontaneity. She's lost her keys. Her list. Her mind. Again. How her tank is always running on empty. How she's always one foot out the door. How when she goes off on a tangent with fire in her eyes you want to kiss her mouth. She drives you crazy. Drives you towards the west coast on a Wednesday morning. Takes over the radio. When you see the scorpion in the sand. See water in the ocean. You watch her in the waves. You know she is at home in the crashing. You worry because she is the water and the wave. She is deep. She is the ocean you willingly drown yourself in each day. She is the salt that softens you. Floats you. Carries you. Heals you.

How she's not afraid to go under. She doesn't mind that you stay on the shore. She is sure your eyes are on her. You'll never admit how much you long to lick the salt from her skin. How she is the best thing you've ever tasted. That your lips want forever with hers. You'd rather drown than say so. You don't have to say it. She feels it. She knows.

You like that she has no expectations except for accepting the here and now. She doesn't believe in fairy-tales or happy endings. You want to prove her wrong.

You love her in ways she's not used to. You know her well. Her sacred spaces. You've studied her long enough to write a thesis on her many faces. What they all mean. Subtleties only a mother should know how to read. You look at her with kaleidoscope eyes. How she was meant to be seen. A wild swirl of colourful chaos. You've made a morning ritual of reading her horoscope to her over coffee. You don't believe in astrology, but you believe in her. You know her ascending, her sun, her moon. After all, she has become your universe.

She's changed the way you look at the sky. The moon is no longer just a moon. The stars are the only diamonds she's ever admired and each night you name one for her. You won't stop until she owns the night. You spend days in bed with your hands never leaving each other's bodies. There is a movie playing that nobody is watching. You can't remember the last time you have eaten. Your fingers memorize her curves and contours. You know the exact shade of brown of her eyes. You make up stories about the people you've seen that day. The man with the round glasses. The woman with the round face.

Sometimes she is still that stranger on the floor but you've learned to lay with her. There are palms on chests and silence. This is no place for words. There are two hearts beating. Morse code. Telling you everything you need to know. You know beside her is where you belong.

ORIGAMI

Instinct calls from the gallows of my gut. Everything in me says no. My patience is growing thinner than these walls. I've heard it all. I fold for you like origami. I write you a poem on scrap paper. Swallow it.

My mouth is a dream catcher. Your mouth is a pseudologue. Sour sleeps on your tongue. Tucked in tight. The clouds sit in the sky like curdled buttercream. You make the mistake of looking for me in the morning.

Why must memory have a scent. My arteries are loaded with tainted blood. An army of arms pulling you away from my heart yet my body still holds you hostage. We are old soul archaic amore that is balancing on the border of an alchemical disaster. We both know this blows up at the end. Here we are.

An artist in love with an arsonist. Your fingers love finding my flaws. Pressing in until I admit I am made from mistakes. I seek asylum in your eyes. You blink and hope I do not notice how long the blue has lived there. I know you want to make room for me. I know you never will. I cannot thrive in cold habitats. Your stubborn will not thaw.

WOMAN

My eyes have a reputation. My eyes are open invitations.
Two brown round portals of temptation. His eyes tell me
it's my touch. Midas. Tongues my finger. My finger cordially
invites him in.

He notices this new woman. The vibrancy. Vibrating high-
frequency woman. Freak woman. The wildling Wild
West woman. Saddle up woman. More Lioness. Priestess.
Goddess than woman.

He gets on his knees to pray to this woman.
Take me in your womb, woman. Let's have more children.
I'd build us a house, but you'd burn it down. Phoenix , woman!

Woman with clay under her nails.
There must be earth in between everywhere.
Ink in my teeth. Paint in my hair. Making what I must.

Awakened woman. The pubic bone. Jaw bone.
The moan that carried across the lake.
Refuses to fake an orgasm woman.

Unpredictable. Unapologetic woman. Barefoot woman.
Lake water woman. Bonfire woman. Lavender and black musk
woman. Fearless woman. Shed skin of the past snake woman.
Life is war. I'm a forever changed woman.

WHEN I SAY 'HERE I AM'

And you hear me.
Finally *see* me.

A hungry spotted cat. The rough tongue. Teeth that will close
on a throat. A mouth open like a baby bird waiting for the
worm; the empty nest.

The quench of a thirsty throat. The small bumps of taste buds
that will never be satiated. Wanton. Feed me watermelon, kiwi,
mango. Sweet summer peaches. Juice. Nectar. Let it drip down
my chin. My legs. Feed me grapes. Grow me a vineyard.
An orchard.

Blame November nights. The empty houses. My mother lies
about the time I was born. I trust no one.
I open my mouth again. My mother falls out. You tell me to
stop cursing in front of the children. *Fuck you.*

I'm buried in the backyard. An accomplice. You know where
my old bones are. You like the new me. Secrets are safe in
selfish mouths.

My eyes are kaleidoscopes. Caves. Caverns.
Fireworks. Vagabonds. Drifters.
How do you teach students not to look at a world
that is trying to teach them everything.

Curious hands that need to make things.
Mistakes. Music. Pottery. Bread.
Bad art. Tie knots. Cast spells. Hold hardened things.
Callus me. I want to remember loving you.

Nights are for Valerian root. Overthinking. Spreading my wings
like that bronze-winged jacana. The hedge sparrow. It's 3:00am
again. I know you are awake. I pray for things.
The moon must think he is a god.

Do you listen now when I say lavender? When my wrists beg
for leather and musk. The sound of the axe splitting the wood.
How thunder rolls under the storm's tongue. When the bird
hits the window. The way you say my name when you cum.

DIG SOUTH

You've settled into this thing now. The groove. The movement. The banter. You can't let her go now. You've never been this close to someone before. Where there is no space between. No end or beginning. Your mouths are one. For this reason, she tells you to run. Fast. Far. If she's heading north, dig south.

You've delicately dug your fingers into her flesh and they have no will to learn anything else. Anyone else. She is eccentric. Aberrant. Apparently, this is what keeps you here. The whiplash. The feet on the dash on Sunday morning drives. You know you should be paying much more attention to the road, and less on how her hair flirts with the wind.

Your heart is as cold as February air. She is the thaw you never saw coming. You love that she hates to cuddle. She swears it's unnecessary. For the needy. You say nothing when she moves closer and folds into your arms like a cashmere sweater. She says she likes it better when your hands are holding her throat. She likes when you bring her to the edge and use your tongue to push her over.

She likes to sit on the throne of her king. Her movements are lyrical. She hypnotises you with her hips and your name slips from her lips and you know you're under her spell for another night. There's no stage fright. The lights are on. She wants you to look at her. No. To see her. She wants your eyes to linger.

She'll never count calories but she will count the seconds that your eyes stay on her. She'll tally the time it took for you to formulate a response. She'll keep track of every evening you don't say good night. You never say good night because there is no good night if she is not there with her nails in your back or her hot breath on your neck.

You want her midnights. All of her mornings. Her eyes are still warning you. "Run. Dig south and don't you dare look for me"

NOVEMBER IS HERE

My chest is on fire. You started it yet your cold heart can't handle the heat. You offer the cold shoulder instead. Smother the flames with indifference. The smoke is insidious. You want water to quench the burn in the back of your throat. It's forgiveness that has never made it past your oesophagus. You're lost in a hiccup. Close your eyes. I wasn't part of the plan. The sky is oil black. The water bearer is banished. Scorpius stings. Run, Orion, run. You start to drive home. The road curves like my hip. You turn around and drive to me. Speeding. Changing lanes without signalling. You never give notice. Not to anyone. Your hands cover my body like moss. I drag my teeth across the nape of your neck. Savage. Collecting samples of your spine beneath my nail beds. Anything to get under your skin. Whisper your secrets into my navel and then call me a whore. I hold my hate behind my teeth. My eyelids. In apothecary jars. In abundance. I spent September sleepwalking so I could see you in my dreams. I woke up. I left you in the thirty one squares of October. Open to the obituaries. I told you … you are dead to me. And now November is here tying knots in my sinking stomach. Not such a subtle weaver. No gossamer threads. No sheepshank or half hitch. Her fingers work feverishly. Carrick bend. Constrictors. She carries in sand disguised as snow. She's shaped like an hourglass. Shoots like a sniper. Trained never to miss her target. One wrong move; I am buried in the white of your bone. And who are you?

METRICS

we moved in moonlight metrics
skin to skin in silver light
back crescent curved
full moon mouthed
the night knew our
never waning want

THESIS

I want to learn you

Study you from
Scalp to sternum
Spine to shin

Begin a thesis
on your thoughts
Become fluent
in your body language

I want to learn you

I WANT YOU IN A WAY

i want you in a way i shouldn't
turn to you like sunflowers turn to the sun

like the shore calls the crest of the wave
crashing into me until we're bent bones and broken

teeth sinking into the endless sea of skin
swells, shells and swallows

all my tongue knows of you
is the salt of your sweat; how you taste of

friday nights; you fuck like a run on sentence
sounding like the last leg of a marathon

fast finish. red fleshed. rubbery. breathless
with bragging rights and feet that ache

with desire

IN ANOTHER WORLD

We wouldn't care that it was a Wednesday
We would wear only bed sheets and each other
We would call in sick
But never get sick of each other
We are too busy falling like lovers do in September
Remembering the scent of one another

My soft mouth would never tire of your hard mouth
We would get wasted and waste the day
Tempting and tiring our tongues
Like we are young and not so high strung
I would read you Neruda in the nude
You would read me e e cummings
Try to get me blushing
Knowing it doesn't take much
more than that to quicken my pulse

My lips would write prose down the stack of your spine
Your hands would work a poem from my hips
I feel your forearm;
Stronger from loving me in these leisurely afternoons
We'd find 69 ways to wait for the moon
and be ready to adore the sky full of stars
no matter how far-fetched they seem

You listen to my west coast dreams
Colorado or the California shore
Until our bodies are fornicating once more
We find ourselves on the hardwood floor
With ease, we would discuss deeper things
such as roots, bones and where rainbows go
and the whereabouts of fathers and other ghosts
and how you know I will never stay

WHAT DO YOU KNOW OF DESIRE

Until it has drenched you.
Stung your lips and made a nest in you.
Wet you with an unmet want.
Pulled you under and possessed you.
Impressed you with its tenacity.
Made your eyes roll back into your head. Blinded you.
Until it has burned the back of your throat. Choked you.
Pulled your teeth out and left your mouth desperate.
Until your heart is a war drum. EDM and Molly at midnight.
A freight train that cannot be stopped. Doesn't want to be.
Until your fingers are nothing more than a forest of pine.
Until your body is moist earth ready for only a potter's hands.
Until the hot breath of a lover is the only kiln that hardens you.
Until you are a delicate vessel waiting to hold the bone broth of
somebody for the sake of finally holding them.
Until you are on a hunger strike;
Your lips and tongue only wanting the curves and corners
of his mouth.
Until you are lost in what he might taste like.
Anise. Old Spice. Malt. Mint.
Until you have withered away to nothing.

STUMBLE

This particular 'I love you'
hangs heavy from my lip
but will not leave
Like the rest of me,
it is stubborn

I try to press it to your lips
so you'll feel what I can't say

I try to get it drunk
so it can stumble home to you
where it belongs

PULLED

He pulled his love from me

 slowly

Like Sunday morning espresso
Like a splinter from a swollen finger
Like weeds from a neglected garden
Like a grey hair from a vain woman's head
Like truth from a liars teeth
Like teeth from a rotten mouth

He pulled his love from me
and left me

in a deep dark nothing

THROW A PARTY FOR HEARTBREAK
(after Mindy Nettifee)

I am half-hearted so the throwing is more of a gentle toss
Like the party is a delicate green garden salad

Your old records spin. Joni paints the party blue.
She sets the mood. I set the table

for one. I'm a medley of numb and denial. I'll force myself
into a smile and my favourite floral dress

from the vintage shop on King street. It hugs my hips
a little too tight. Your arms are phantom limbs

tonight. The punch will be hard.
Spiked with Silent Sam. I'll probably drink

too much. Isn't that what I was to you?
All noise and nonsense? This is the consequence

of wearing my heart on my sleeve. Believing
your cold heart could care. It is a sad soiree

of sorts. Only the hostess and your ghost. I toast
the shrinking balloons as they slowly deflate

into metaphors. I pop them with my teeth
Offering a kindness I wish I knew.

THE ART OF FORGETTING

Salt the wounds but unseason their name. Make it bland. Bury it under your tongue. Soon you will forget the taste. Open your hands. Stop holding on. You cannot hold a ghost or anything else that disappears. Unlearn the lyrics to that song. That melody. Make your heart beat to something else. Pin the petals back on the daisy. He never loved you. Turn the inside jokes right side out. Forget how they made you laugh. Forget how you loved hiding in the dark spots of their mouth. Meditate them into a distant memory. Find a spot to tuck away the almosts. Place the in-betweens somewhere you cannot see. The spine. Make them vanish. Banish them beneath each vertebrae. Use your magic. Houdini them out of your hippocampus. Make them your keys. Your sunglasses. The reason you walk into the kitchen at night. Or anything else you so easily forget. Sometimes loving someone is like riding a bike. Or swimming. Or breathing. It's impossible to unlearn something that has settled into your bones… or someone that has made a home in your marrow. Roll up the mat. Let them know they are no longer welcome. Soon they will become an unwanted solicitor. You no longer answer the door for anyone you do not know.

TOAST

time heals everything
show me a shaman
in a sweat lodge
with two arms spinning
in circles
perhaps
he is disguised as an old man
who makes me wet
who makes me forget
for a moment
while our souls collide
like two cars
going too fast on the interstate
too late
we've escaped our bodies
we're a couple of naughty
ghosts dancing on the side of the road
we're avocado and toast
my overripe millennial
spread on top
of your wholewheat basic bottom
somehow it works
everyone is eating it up
until it's gone
time is just something
we put in the toaster

MUD POOLS

I count the minutes before I lose him to the hands of
midnight.
He becomes a star. A wish.

I sleep to dream of spring; crocuses and him
opening up.

He tells me my eyes are wells; No.
He tells me my eyes are brown
mud pools he needs to drown in.

He tells me he is the bearer of water and bad news.
He does not know how to swim, yet he knows me well.
Tilts my head to pour his knowledge down my soft throat.

He says he wants to salt my lips and kiss them crimson.
That he loves my skin but considers my arms a prison.

He tells me he doesn't want to learn how to hold me.
Not without an escape route. He needs to be a bullet
that leaves an exit wound.

He tells me I'm a beautiful mess. That I look my best
when dressed only in moonlight. Silver spilling across my
breasts. That is when we wear the night out.

He wants to love in privacy. Have the intimacy
that is found between the bee and the honeysuckle.

Tells me he wants it bare knuckle.
Knee-jerk natural with unclench jaws.
We cannot grind our teeth. Only our greedy bodies.

He tells me my mouth is acid rain.
He is a rock. He is a rock. He is a rock.
It takes time.

I count the minutes. My arms become midnight.
I dream of spring.

INTERRUPTED

let me be a woman;

interrupted

say something
say a thing
anything

your teeth
have ancient tree roots
i want to pull them out

one by one
ones through sevens
rock them gently
watch them lift
little by little
right before they leave
their soft pink nest

offer me something
from your mouth
that i don't have to pull

CRUX

The parts of me that fit into the parts of you.
How warm breath can carve a name into a collarbone
so it stays forever. Whatever that is.
The way I fit into the crook of your elbow
could almost be called cliché.
Eyes that dance with mine from across the room
giving my capillaries a reason to bloom
and break across my face.
Burn up my neck.
Desire crawls through me like a hungry predator.
You tongue my wrists before you tie them.
Yes. I'm still here.
You're still here. We are courageous.
The same way we are cowards.
Tonight, brave my body like open land.
Let your hands become nomads.
This is when a kiss is never just a kiss.
Our lips get lost in this sloppy precision of taking and
tasting what we want.
I have been waiting for you to know me.
Like this. This sweaty bliss. We stick like honey. Simple syrup.
It's so much more complicated than that.
This is the one thing we are sure of.
Your eyes are coloured a shade of sadness
I have never seen before.
There are things caught in my throat.
I am saving the saying of them for a rainy day.

TASTE OF NOSTALGIA

Our memories are savoury. Something I can hold
on my tongue. Yesteryears taste like a tincture of tin,

burnt toast and lost time. This mouth has collected
a carnival of crumbs. A merry-go-round of morsels that

mercilessly spin and spin   and spin. A haunted house
of cardamom, cumin and confessions. The dizzy dancing

of daydreams along the insides of my cheek. The ache of
nostalgia as it nests into the notches of my teeth.

THE ACHE
(after Mahogany L. Browne)

I've known it in places named
teeth, temple, arch of foot
It has dug talons into the trenches of my bones
Making itself known with every bend
of wrist or elbow

I've known it to bite with dull teeth
Lock its jaws around the what-ifs
I've known it to live in my lower back
Stretch around to my groin
Grow into a beast called *active labour*
Let's out a long howl

I've witnessed it in ice cream cones
Street signs. Smells something like a gin soaked ghost
you can't ignore. Thrives in naive spaces
Slaps my face then walks away
I've known it to always leave

So - leave

Unstick from my ribs. Stop swelling.
Stop making a nest in my mouth and singing;
taking up space created by the absence
of a name

BUTTERFLY GARDEN

i take everything you say
with a grain of salt. i am as seasoned as the dead

sea. bones brined. holding water
instead of you. i am unrefined. i love you

with a lead foot. all in. lock jaw. greedy as the lioness
licking the last morsel from the leg

of the antelope. i am a narcissist. you are the mirror. a shiny
silver thing. a pin. a beating red balloon

lives in my chest. i had high hopes. planted a butterfly garden
in february. if only march had wings. had vertebrae.

i am a clay body. moving with memory. turning
towards you. asking your fingers to open me. widen

the hollow. pull me into a vessel you pour
your vanity into. drink from my thin lips.

DRIFTWOOD

We held it in our chest, didn't we

The want was bergamot and butterfly winged
Monarchs ruling what rests behind our rib

cage. Pretending not to flutter. A muttering
of the superfluous. The superficial. Sometimes

the supermoon. A recycling of sidereal months.
Riding the same storm. Waiting for the rain

to talk about the weather. We no longer speak about
who is buried in the garden. You no longer wait for rain

that goes rogue. Facts: You cannot feel. I felt you
fall through my fingers like wet seeps through the cracks

of a faulty flat roof. Stealthy. Slowly. Almost like you weren't.
Until I am standing in a flooded kitchen. Like I never lived

here. It was always all or nothing. I am driftwood.

YOU SAY YOU WANT ME

Like you've had me before

Like you know me

You say it like you always get everything
you say you want

You want my fingers to wrap firmly around you
As if you could tell me which fingertip holds the memory
of being sliced open by the thin yellow metal
of a measuring tape

You want to know the shape and shade of my breasts
To caress the curves that will not fill your hands
As if deflated balloons are as fun as the after party

You want to part my thighs
As if you won't notice the signs of the stretching it took
to become the woman

you want

Perhaps you can have my body
If you can tell me the wars it has waged
How I've earned my stripes
The plum purple lines on my legs
Delicately decorated with iridescent indents
Little silkworms climbing

If you can tell me how old I was
when eight staples sealed a small section of my stomach shut
An operating room epiphany; you can survive
without certain parts of your body

If you can tell me the time my
daughter was cut out of me; caesarian style
If you can tell me she was breech
Yellow and three weeks early

If you can tell me how many stitches I needed
after I pushed out my son

Would you still want me?

My lips are
exit sign above the back door
four corner stop sign
slow burn fire
red

You show up with your hose in hand
A soft mattress for landing

You think you're the hero

I know you're not
brave
enough
to burn with me

REMEMBER
(after Joy Harjo)

Remember when I swam in the silk of your eyes.
Grey glass lakes. I almost drowned. Remember

Sending electric currents down my spine.
You have eels for fingers. Defibrillator palms. Remember

You brought me back to life that night and I'm living
without you; My mouth closes like a morning glory.

Remember the taste of September. The spill and burn
of botanicals. How lovesick sits as a nervous lump in a throat;

Remember nothing was real that night except everything. A
tryst of twisted stalk. Define the taste of wild cucumber.

That is all there is to remember.

SORRY

Sorry about the blood. The bleeding. It wouldn't stop.
Just like the snow. The snowfall. The snowflake.

You warned me that tomorrow might be warm.
As if someone as cold as you would know anything
about melting.

HOPE

verb
\ 'hōp \
: *to cherish a desire with anticipation : to want something to happen or be true*

Hope might find a stick figure silhouette taking a six figure salary to bed and planning an early retirement. Hope hangs on stars. Hides between birthday candles and in daily horoscopes. Hope believes in soul mates. Hope is a dopamine drip. Hope has the optimists planting tulip bulbs in the fall while the pessimist plants plastic flowers in their garden or doesn't plant anything at all. Hope dares her feet to climb the fortress of walls you've built around your heart. Hope is a mouth that says yes. Desperate for dialogue. Despair leaves a certain scent in the air. Hope lets it linger.

Lana wrote a warning; 'hope is a dangerous thing for a woman like me'. Hope is a thing we cannot hold, but here we are, trying. Hope is the grenade. The pin. The pull. Hope is that you'll still love me to pieces. While the pieces of me are mangled and barely recognizable. We hold hope in our palms and call it prayer. For this reason, I do not hold hands. What am I holding when I'm holding you? Not hope. Not the future. I know now that you can hold nothingness. My fingers have become familiar with what fleeting feels like. I'm a masochist with a matchstick and a mouthful of kerosene. Hoping you'll kiss me. That is what hope will do to someone like me.

Taylor sings 'shake it off'. Like I haven't tried like a big, wet dog to shake you off of my skin. Like when Annie Lennox sings 'No More "I Love You's'. She knows. You're the sensei of the silent treatment. I'm still learning to listen. I'm a hopeless disciple. My mouth is yours. Use your skill set. Take my teeth. My tongue. Take what you need from me. Anything that will stop the taste of disappointment from sliding down my throat. A woman like me is planting tulips, waiting for Spring and saying I love you.

*Reference to Lana Del Ray 'Hope Is A Dangerous Thing',
Taylor Swift 'Shake it Off' and Annie Lennox 'No More I Love You's'

SOUR MILK

Stay with me until the milk turns sour
Until the hours fall off the face of the clock
Until the last crocus crawls through small rocks and soil
Until the arctic ocean comes to a soft boil
Until the whiskey is ready to bottle
Until we can chew the philosophies of Plato and Aristotle
Until they've rebuilt Babylon, the citadel, Athens, Rome
Until every vagabond and hermit crab finds a home
Until the snail slides his belly-foot body across the end of time
Until each and every last leech is full of blood
Until the Sahara floods and lends its sand to every hourglass
Stay until the milk turns sour

COMMA

my friend, the comma
not concerned with melodrama
only the importance of

                                                    a pause

LBD

When winter comes
Let me be the tree
that drops its leaves
like a little black evening dress

You'll find me
naked and gnarled
with reaching limbs
not able to resist the sky

DECEMBER IS A DANCE AND I HAVE TWO LEFT FEET

The sky would have been different had the rainbow
crowned a day later; Everything would have.

I could have caught a fish. Gutted it. Swallowed.
Had it inside me. Who needs air to breathe?

A coward circles the sun 48 times. Cannot find his tongue.
Cuts it on the witching hour. Spills sour semen.

Holds on to demons. A grudge like a lover.
Will not smudge the ghost out.

Drinks the moon, whole, only while warm.
I stand stark naked in new snow.

You are winter. December is a dance. I surrender.
I never thought I could love the cold.

A SIGH AS A SONG

It's this day in December
The year the world decided to end
I'm sitting in the ashes

I never noticed before how far the field stretches
Like arms of a languid lover
Half lit by the soft white of Christmas lights

I turn my back on the world
The fingernail of the moon finds my hip
Digs in. Doesn't let go. Like a leech

I'm curled like a cat
A feline that will not align with your ludicrous mind
A mother always feels the let down

My sigh is carried by the wind
A certain susurrus of despair
A soft morning song. A song of mourning

TEWS FALLS IN WINTER

on a perfect first date
there would be no talking

only moaning

coming

from too tall trees; hair pulled
by the wind. any bare skin

would be bitten
by frost. small raised peaks

in the distance. we would be high
above the valley. a stretching of long legs

belonging to the river running
through. a white glistening across the belly

of the forest. a mad rush of wet
spilling over the edge

BILIRUBIN

The year is yellow and young
January is jaundice; coddled

This year is already crawling
Feeling for new teeth with her tongue

EVERYTHING IS DIFFERENT HERE

The way the house moans and clicks
Morning crashes in like cymbals
The sunrise is a red brick wall

We're temporary intruders
The bread doesn't rise and the fruit rots
Crumbs confetti the floor

The bed is borrowed. The mattress is hard and old
Not the first time I've laid on a metaphor
Find me on the floor tonight instead

Perspective is a gift; A mindset shift

Mourning crashes in like a white accordion
The sunrise is young blood on a highway

Transfusions. Confusion.
Insurance needs to know when you went over the median

Clipped wings of the nightingale. His nocturnal tune cut short
Compassion is fleeting and small. I say nothing at all
My teeth become thickets full of ticks and chokecherry

Everybody is in it now. After assessment it's safe to assume
it's a cesspool of collective drowning. We're frowning as we try
to swim inside of a dying whale. The underbelly is swollen

MARY OLIVER EYES

Take me to where the wind is an ocean
waving through the trees
Where cedars creak and sway and talk
to me in a way no person ever has
I want the bark and the bite
The break of a branch
The bend of a river

Canopy me in shades of green
Give me the slow buzz of the bumblebee
Humble me with the crack of
bramble and underbrush underneath my feet

Lend my ears to the chirp and trill
from little bodies of birds
The quiet of the cattle
Let crickets woo with their wing song
along the flora and fauna
Let the pines creak like floorboards
welcoming me home

TOMORROW IS A PLACE
(after Sanna Wani)

Where we foster a forest. Suckle sap from the trees. Learn to stand taller. Lean into the sway. My steps and my voice become softer. *Softer.* Time holds me in his arms. We dance the slowest dance. He points at the swans. The swing hung from the walnut tree. The landscape that is frosted like a cake. The window from which I would watch the moon curl into the darkness. Time whispers *'remember'* like I would all-too-soon forget the curve of the road that always took me home. Where is home if a heart is in between places? It is where this exhale can finally be birthed and we can dry our faces by the hearth. Unpack the boxes. Take in the view. Paint the walls and call it ours. Tomorrow is a place we live in.

BUNGALOW

This bungalow
has more than one story

A narrative like a split hair
As open as a sewing needle head

The walls hold a sound
ripe with vowels

Words that rot and crawl through
the cavities of where we live

Secrets are whispered and
bend like a spineless serpent

The belly bows with sacrifice
The sorrows of tomorrow

The hiss of an echo slides
through the body of eternity

ABODE

it's just bricks and mortar
it's nothing more than
four walls and an unfinished basement
where the mice and water get in

it's just the tile and paint we picked out
before we knew all about
aesthetics and cosmetics and how
you cannot make a home within bad bones

it's just a roof made of shingles
there isn't one single
moment that could tell us how well
we were under cover from one another

it's just a cast iron bathtub
where one could scrub
the day off her skin
a place to begin understanding the drain

it's just a house
it's just
a
house

CLOSING THE COUNTRY HOME

Emptiness echoes
The sounds are not mine
They come from small mouths
I watch the sun fall behind
the trees one last time

Time stretches the shadows across the lawn
The sky lets out a blood orange yawn

Who will now swing from the walnut tree
We gave it our all, didn't we?

If the walls could talk...
what would they whisper to the new ones?

'You'll be happy here...Most of the time.
Most of the time, you'll be happy.
The kitchen is for dancing and burning love.
The bedrooms are for silly stories and sleepless nights.
The small wall beside the closet is the best for marking heights.
The moon is different out here. The sun too. You'll see.
You'll welcome the longer roads.
The quiet is so loud if you just listen. Just be.'

A FIELD GUIDE TO SURVIVING
A POSTAGE STAMP SIZED SUBURBAN BACKYARD

Observe the fence. Find

a weed. Call her wild

flower. Call her baby

blue eyes. Call her sweet

pea. Call her poppy. Pull

the pink from her petal

cheek. Pay attention to

how the dew drops

dance on her black round

mouth. Spread her

seed. Plan her escape.

THIS SATURDAY STARTS DIFFERENTLY

We are up
They are down
There is coffee. A silent sun

spilling onto the table
punctuated by the pink insides
of a grapefruit

We remember how bright and warm
a morning can be

MANDUKASANA

This is where I let go of all the things I hold in my hips
The men who have lived there
The heaviness of my babies and their hungry mouths

This is where I cut the strings of the taut hammock
The hesitant sway
The anchor of a groin that carries gradients of grief

This is where it is safe to widen; to take up room
The room disappears
The world leaves my shoulders

This is where the floor allows my bones to fall through
The spine is forgiving
The exhale leaves me full

THINGS I LEFT ON MY MAT
(after Tonight's Yoga Practice)

Three pairs of shoes. The front porch
swing. The swinging. The murder

of crows. Crying in the night.
Two central incisors that will never meet.

Diastema. The card for the orthodontist.
Places are pleading to be crowded.

Need an escape room. The open front door
is obvious. The squid-like leech shoulder

hold of the obsequious. The sideways shuffle
of the snake. The blink of 3 a.m. I let it go.

Leave it like it never was. Like we were never
in the same mouth. Like you taught me, dear teacher.

A LETTER HOME

I think it's the way I don't fit in here. Anywhere, really.
The lawns are more manicured than my hands. There are
mourning doves and sunrises I cannot see. My eyes have
no choice but to drink the juice of the magnolia trees and
black mulch.

There was a bobcat next door. Never showing its teeth.
Pushed enough growl through the fence to dare me back
inside. Fool. Not even the fat cold rain could bully me
back in. Flood and I will swim to where I belong.

I need to tend to the weeds and wildflowers. My walnut tree.
To be back where the grass could stretch its long arms and I
could witness the day yawn yellow. Where the night could be
naked and the stars were never shy. I need the quiet Neruda
knows of. 12 seconds.

My belongings are in a shipping container. Light it on fire.
Use this poem to start it. Strike a match against my useless
teeth. Let there be light to guide me home.

GOOD MOTHER

i wanted to be a good mother

who doesn't wonder about the knife
cutting through the warm butter

of a wrist. a witness of softer things. one
who will not always envy the bent back

of an archer's bow or the speed of an arrow.
one who knows of the apple seed. the tireless deed

of a becoming the tree stump. growing from nothing. planning
blindfolded future. keep speaking of hope like it has hands

for holding. bones are not silt that can settle. maybe it was
more metallic. more of a chlorinated foreign body. i forget

the taste of freedom. time is a pirate. patience is lost
at sea. a sailor lives in my angry mouth. i wanted

to want to chew the worm. greet your open beak. give you
wings and honesty. without pushing; wait for the empty nest.

someone needs to fly. to be more than a night-fevered
daydreamer. more than a wanton wanderlust-laced woman

with a burning throat. travelling light. catching the next flight to
phoenix to watch an arizona sunset. to be born.

again. i wanted to be a good mother.
i wanted this and more.

MINIVAN

This poem is about the minivan.
The orange glow of the gas light. How the brakes grind.
This poem reminds me to book an oil change.
That the winter tires can now come off.
This poem questions the make, the mileage and how much
longer the van can go before it is a broken down thing on the
side of the road.
This poem wonders about the selling of spare parts
and scrap metal;
If any of it will be salvageable. Worth anything -
If there will be anything left at all.
This poem is (not) about the minivan.

STATUS UPDATE
(after Rebecca Lindenburg)

Samantha Heeley is up early again. Remembers she cannot
watch the sunrise from here. Her heart sinks like a red brick.
The kind they use to build these cookie cutter homes.
Samantha is not at home. She is in a house. Samantha is
exhausted and drinking coffee. Is overthinking. Samantha is
admiring the freckles that are finding a place on her son's face.
Notices her husband has shaved his beard. Notices his mouth
for the first time. Samantha makes a to-do list. Workout. Yoga.
Paint. Breathe. Samantha Heeley is procrastinating. Again.
Samantha changes her toddler's diaper. Adds potty-training to
the to-do list. Changes over a load of laundry. Changes her
mind. Closes her eyes and daydreams she is a twenty-something
in Tuscany instead of a thirty-seven year old in purgatory.
Samantha Heeley takes something out for dinner. Again.
Daydreams of a life where her children aren't picky eaters.
Daydreams of a life where children aren't. Looks into her
daughter's deep brown eyes. Feels the guilt deep in her
gut. Samantha's teeth break

through the skin of an apple. Samantha stares into
space. Samantha's eyes become UFOs. Samantha regrets
opening her big mouth, making you an alien. Samantha has
become a 'stay-at-home mom'. Samantha misses work. The
scrubs. The extraction of teeth, the blood and bravery.
Samantha paints another bird. Experiences an absurd wing
envy. Flaps her arms in a furious fashion. Samantha curses
gravity and circumstance. Samantha does a dance
with impostor syndrome. Folds another load of laundry.

Samantha steps outside. Allows the lips of the sun to land on her collarbone. Samantha is sunburnt and smiling. Samantha has a sudden urge to purge the junk drawers. The closets. To run away. Samantha Heeley wants to laugh so hard that sound no longer comes out and it still hurts the next day. Samantha wants to paint her lips and the town red. Head out to the local bar. Listen to the man with his acoustic guitar. His gruff voice crawling through the speaker. Samantha wants to sing along. Dance to live music. To feel alive again. Samantha folds another load of laundry.

WHEN THERE ARE NO WORDS, ONLY PLANT NAMES AS METAPHORS
(After Tony Hoagland)

I want to tell you things
always
in the thick middle of the night

Morning comes up empty. There are no words for this
unbecoming. For believing you are a winged thing. One must
first be the caterpillar. A chrysalis.

'Desire' is pastel. Monotone. I want a word that will catch fire
once it leaves my lips. There is no such word that describes
how my fingers want to become arachnids. Crawl all over your
body. Lay eggs underneath your skin.

There is no word for the emptiness. That void when someone
takes a small part of you when they leave. This hollow has no
name. It is the womb from which poetry is born.

What is the opposite of wanderlust? Sometimes I want to tell
you things. Like I want to stay right here and watch the clouds
curl. Stay long enough to plant a garden.

WEATHERVANES AND WINDCHIMES

the bone glass windchime
sings a church choir song cutting
the buttery breeze

bloodstained morning sky
bellyache of cloud bottoms
warning crawls through grass

WISHBONES

my body is all wishbones and want
your promise is propaganda
belief is bold cold dead bolt
eyes not letting me in
obsidian skies
show me your teeth
open throat
swallow
me

UNSULLIED

unmask my mouth and kiss me like the
toes of the world are balancing
on top of a glass marble
like i am unsullied
i am a grease fire
out of control
put me out
with your
lips

BORDERLINE BOREDOM

i become an astronaut
in your moon mouth
needing oxygen
more time
here
time has no hands
only bodies becoming
shooting stars

POEM BEGINNING WITH A RETWEET
(after Maggie Smith)

If you aren't in an intimate relationship with
the sky you see from your house every single day

If your pulse isn't somersaulting
with want writhing between your legs

If you aren't observing the underwing of the falcon,
the pause of a pupa, the direction of the wind

If you're not barefoot, a little bit broken
and breathing it all in

what's the point?

Italics indicate the retweet

THINGS I WANT TO BE SURROUNDED BY WHEN I'M DYING ON MY DEATHBED
(after @lord_birthday)

Spice the room with thyme and clover. Before my days are
over, I have one last request for a rainbow sorbet sunset.
A string quartet playing in the corner. The belly dance of a
candle flame. Paint pallets and pinched pots. Plants
that say 'we made it this far'. A cheese platter. No. I'm dying so
please make that a four course charcuterie board. With feta and
figs. The really good Spanish olives. I'm dying and I'm greedy.
I want a thunderstorm that is full of ego. That shakes the
window. I want smiles from familiar teeth. I want your eyes so
I can drown forever in green seas. I want my babies. Their
warm breath on my cheek. I want everyone I've ever loved -
let's make this room a little crowded, shall we?

THE QUIET I KNOW

The quiet I know hides in plain sight.
In the dark corner of Carlisle nights.
It is the stillness that lies on top of the lake in Maberly.
It is in the deep belly of Muskoka woods.

The quiet I know hangs in the
hospital air when baby moves from womb to room;
A mother's breath held captive until her child cries
for the first time and shatters the stoic air.

The silence I know hides
in the silk of monarch wings and milkweed.
Mouths that you wish it wouldn't.
In the pockets of two a.m.

There is back-of-the-church quiet. Library quiet.
Tibetan Monk quiet. Underwater quiet.
Once-the children-are-finally-in-bed-quiet.
The hide-your-deepest-darkest-secret quiet.

There is the silence that sleeps on the floor
right after you've poured out your big truth.
Sharpens its teeth. Becomes the deafening roar.
The lion's mouth that swallows every sound.

There is a quiet I don't know - yet - that I want to love
insidiously and inside out until it's loud again. A silence I want
desperately enough that I stalk it in dark alleyways and empty
parking lots until it becomes the quiet I know.

BIRCH BARK

the birch bark curled
like black smoke
like an angry upper lip
like the toes of a lover

NOCTURNE

I become limbless behind the eyelid
Free fall through the onyx of nights pupil

Twilight is the stillness I want
to swim in; become a torso in black tar

The sky is a collapsed lung
of a young love. Stars are only anyone

you've ever cared for. Ceremoniously
This is where the bough breaks

the jaw of morning. A plate of
porcelain begs for parting clouds

I WILL LOVE YOU
(after The Beatrice Letters, Lemony Snicket)

Obsessively. Sometimes. Always. I will love you sugar sweet. I
will love you like plaque loves the neck of a tooth. I will love
you like the paper tooth loves the artist. Like an artist loves a
blank canvas. How a blank canvas loves the cool lick of acrylic.
How the paint brush becomes the tongue and the canvas
becomes the lover. I will love you like the neck of a lover
craves a bite. I will love you like a potter's hands love the
speckled clay body. The wet. The opening and pulling. The
glossy glazed finish after the firing; when the hands are finished
working. I will love you until the hands of the moon push the
tides away. I will love you like a tired mother loves her first sip
of coffee and stretch marks love to leave their mark on a
mother's hips. I will love you like a garden loves good dirt. Like
the garden loves the coneflower. I will love you like the
goldfinch loves the coneflower in the garden. Until the sun is
no longer gold and does not wake to dance across the meadow
in the morning. I will love you like the weathervane loves the
west wind. Like the weatherman loves to be wrong. How the
wind loves to ruin an otherwise perfect picnic. Stubbornly. Like
the grass stain loves a denim knee. Like the red of a cabernet
loves a mother-in-law's white carpet. I will love you until all the
greediness gives back. I will love you like a bear paw loves a
salmon stream. Until the salmon fly and the streams all run dry.
I will love you until the last Taurus is no longer stubborn. I will
love you impossibly and when you are being impossible and
because you love me because I am impossible and that counts
for something. I will love you until the road runs out, the gas
runs out and I run out of words that tell you I will love you like
this.

WHAT I AM TAKING

*"I was always ashamed to take. So I gave. It was not a virtue.
It was a disguise." Anaïs Nin*

I am taking the apple from the throat of Adam
I will take my time with the taking

I am taking back each time I made myself smaller
I am taking back each time I made myself quiet
I am taking steps in the right direction
I am taking deeper breaths
I am taking notes
I am taking time for myself
I am taking back the parts of me I gave away
I am taking back every minute that had you in it

I am taking it all and
I will be greedy

MAY FOURTH

You knew I would look for you
in fields of mayflowers and four leaf covers

This time I brought my field notes;
Privy to displays of invertebrates and other toxic things

The sun is a round mouth of gold teeth
I too, am a rooted thing, refusing to rot

A POEM PROMPTED BY THE LICENCE PLATE ON THE VEHICLE THAT CUT ME OFF

Jolted by the rhetoric. Bold blue letter bullets.
A loaded question;

 '*RU HAPPY*'

It was a little too early for a red light
interrogation. Too late for litigation.
Cement dries. Holds up a fence.
What will you make of a broken wing?

I swallow the sharp points of an N
Let the roundness of the O slowly slip
down the back of my throat.

I drive to the post office. Mail the letter.
Return home to make dinner.

Ballet is beautiful
at the cost of a ballerina's foot.

PALINODE

I apologized/once
for the bleeding/ and the snow

Never again
will I say sorry
for the way the softness of my heart
hides behind the shape of my potter's ribs

MAKING SMALL TALK WITH STRANGERS AT BARS

I tell you I'm from Wichita or Wyoming. Somewhere less
boring than this place. Your face looks like it has lived one
thousand lives before this one. I'd want to pin you as the
conniving type but your eyes tell me otherwise.
You come close enough to drown me in Drakkar Noir.
The chokehold of nostalgia. You tell a lame joke that has
my attention. You drink your domestic draft as I rattle off
reasons to be reckless. To live like we have the lifespan
of a housefly.
You're enough of a stranger so I tell you that I sit in darkness
sometimes. You tell me we could make shadows. I tell you my
body is a flame. I wouldn't blame you for turning away
but you stay and you say you would rather be a house fly
than a barfly. I look you straight in the eye and say
*"what matters most is how well you walk through the fire"**
You look at me with intrigue and desire.
You say you know these words. I call you a liar.
You ask what I'm drinking and if I'd like another.
I tell you I am drunk on life and that I'm somebody's wife
and somebody's mother. We stand in the awkwardness
slowly sipping on the silence and side glances. I tell you
that it's about time I get home. You say you're getting used
to being alone like loneliness is something somebody should
get used to.

Bukowski quote

CONTEMPLATING GIVING UP COFFEE

How do I give you up
when I carry you in my yellowed teeth

You are the dark sun that opens my eyes
and sets sail in my chest

How do I teach my hands
not to reach for you in mornings light

for fear there may come a day
that I forget the taste of you

tiptoeing across my tongue
I have never been one to let go

of what I love

RAINBOW LAKE

Blessed is this little lake and the long winding road to get to
it. The red fox. The red winged blackbirds. The red wine in the
cardboard box. The red stretch of horizon. The hungry hawk.
The heron. The drumroll of the downy. The chickadees tender
trill. The diamonds dancing on liquid indigo. The croak
creeping from the camouflaged frog. The sunfish. The sun. The
slow dig of the snapping turtle. The luna moth. The doe. The
opening of the daffodils. The almost broken bench. The turtle
in the middle of the road. The moss that cloaks the rock. The
turkey tail. The burn of birch bones. The hill of rolling rock.
Jane's limited edition library. The legend of the whip-poor-will.
Blessed is the calm before the storm.

SILVERY LANE

The table is set with silver
intentions. Forks in the road
lead me to the falling place
where grace is a perfect white cloud.

A storm is coming to salt the sky. Thunder rolls
out the red carpet. The black ceiling cracks
like a pubescent voice. Ask me again about
the star dust in the mason jars.

Night is haunted by the shrill
trill of the whippoorwill. Her call
creeps through the window. Wants
to make a widow out of me.

Lake wakes while we sleep. Moon slips
behind the pines. Loon haunts the lazy morning
mist. Bird beak finds the worm the fish wants. Want
has wings. Buzzes like a beady fly. Greedy as a buzzard.

Heart expands like a frog's vocal sac. Jumps.
Pumps faster. Want lurches from the loins. Lower lip
holds time like tobacco. Lover holds lower lip
like a prisoner. Goes through like a hook.

This mouth is a whispering peony. Round pink bud.
Be a night ant. Open me. Fiddlehead to fern. Be relentless
as a rabid raccoon. Sunday sermon slow. Yin. Vinyasa.
Morning comes; I plant gratitude in the garden.

MILK GLASS

maybe my bones were more milk glass
your hands more barbarian
your teeth more barbed wire
always insisting on immediacy

your tongue
recluse
red light asleep
in the middle
of the street
in the middle
of the night

your mouth
spoiled clam
dead muscle

your eyes
void
vulture
ventriloquist

our cheek to cheek
was a weak attempt
at closeness

your collar bone
concrete
albeit
your softest part

CLOSURE

We speak of closure
like peace lies in the teeth
of a zipper

like the wound isn't a gaping
piece of Tupperware
with no fitting lid to be found

like your breath isn't the coldest
winter wind crawling under
the bedroom door at night

Like my parched lips could stay
sealed shut and not drink
the water you bear

THE PHARMACIST

White coat with salt-
and-pepper hair
Tired, pale eyes
Asks if I have any questions
Any allergies
Confirms my birthday
Asks …. 'Scorpio?'
Says he knows my type.
Knew. Has an ex. Or was it two.
Says he still feels
the sting
I smile.
Of course you do
We have a reputation
for a reason
The pharmacist takes
my arm to fill
with Pfizer
Warns me
it might sting

WILTED

Love me like the fire in my belly loves dancing
Give in to me like the bent back
of a blue collar man

Love me summer solstice long
Red hot, relentless and leaving
my limbs buttery soft
like a pile of limp
boston lettuce
leaves wilting
in the
sink

HOMESICK

I fold
the napkin
into an airplane
a crane
a boat

Make an accidental waterway
with the tears
I didn't know were coming

Love unroots a heart
Unsettles it
Promises a new start

I pinch
my inner thigh
under the old table
in the new kitchen
and make plans for tomorrow

FORECAST

Like the sky is all wild woman
Her hunger sitting deep in her belly
Opening to an endless obsidian
Opening like a lion's mouth
Letting a roar leap out
that echoes like a head
hitting pavement on
a quiet street

POTTER

with her
hands and
her fire

both clay
and man

harden

DEVASTATED WOMAN KNOWS SHE'LL NEVER BE AS BEAUTIFUL AS BANFF NATIONAL PARK
*(*after 'The Onion' headline)*

even with her ink pot eyes
her springs, hot

snowy white peaks
pointing skyward

a persistent body
constantly moving

a basin mouth holding blues
a rock flour illusionist

FAIRLIGHT

We live here now
Where the water body does a belly dance

Rolling into the evening wake
An orange-tipped offering to the sinking sky circle

We witness slow-motion monarch wings
while our lungs fill with heady lavender air

Our new blood is offered on the front porch
until our swollen pink skin tells a story of the thirsty north

Red heads. White tails. Blue cans
leave us with Wednesday morning hangovers

We paint the hallway ghost white
and let the river elbow lead us home

GROWTH

Morning crawls out of my throat in groggy foggy fashion
Filaments of the freckled night before splinter my eyelid.
We've had conversations harder than concrete.
Pinwheeled and peeled back. Mule-mouthed. Ox-tongued.

Love lasting as long as the heavy head of a peony. A heavy sigh.
A summer. We want the tomorrows to be a weed. We plant the
seed in our night pillows. Hope for the growth of an invasive
species in the soil of time. Place a cracked clawfoot bird bath in
the west corner.

What we call love leaves me with swollen glands. Hands that
are perennials. I will name you a colour. Write you on scrap
paper. Chew you and hide you in my throat's attic. Build your
walls up higher. Your ancient tree rings. You were made to
climb.

I'll bite your lip when you say leave. Call you a liar until love is
the answer. The cancer that swims in our veins. Like we've
rehearsed, it will be my heart in the hearse. Dress me in black.
Open casket. Look at me . Write my eulogy on a hosta leaf you
pull from the yellowing plant in the garden that was never rich
enough to witness growth.

SOME SUMMERS

Give me a summer that is gruelling. Hot heat

you can see rising from the street sticking

to your teeth. Clouds so grounded they drag

their feet. Give me a gritty city graffiti

scavenger hunt. Twilight park picnic

until we smell like we cut summer

across the twist of her wristed stem

Nothing remotely modest

Only bottles of midnight honesty

and intoxicated galaxies

YOU CAN'T HAVE IT ALL
(after Barbara Ras)

But you can have small things.
Like the lid of an acorn. A chickadee feeding from your hand.
The smile from a stranger. The pale pink of an orchid you've
kept alive. Hope. The white top of a dandelion. A wish. Or
three. You name them. They are your children. The beat of a
heart on an ultrasound. An infant's mouth at your breast. The
hand of a baby holding onto your finger for dear life.

You can have simple things. You can have birch-barked
friends. Birdsong. The wind whispering secrets in your ear
while kissing your neck. You can have the place where the wild
cucumber grows and the cattle roam. You can dig your hands
into the earth. Grow food from seed. Have a place to watch the
corn stalks sway slowly as the day fades away. You can have the
night sky and who could want more than this?

You can have sleepy Sunday mornings. Real orgasms. A lover
that knows the tenderness of the inside of your thigh. A
tongue that knows saffron and good wine. You can crack the
spine of a new book. Your knuckles. You can have a friend
whose laughter melts the rest of the world away. You can have
eyes that touch your soul and teach you what mediocre is. You
can have a heart that never settles.

You can have the tug of nostalgia. The yellow of your grandmother's kitchen. A closet full of Fresca. The red tile of your Nonna's dining room where your childhood lived. How something as simple as tomatoes could smell so good. The sound of a sewing machine. You can have a dog named Lady that loved being in your arms, even when she was dying. A park swing designated for after work underdogs from a father who worked too much. A mother who just *knows* by your voice. Who says 'I'm sorry...I was so sick'. You can have a hug that finally feels like a forever home.

You can't have it all, but you can have all of this.

Art: Samantha Heeley

"I have to be rent and pulled apart and live according to the demons and the imagination in me. I'm restless. Things are calling me away. My hair is being pulled by the stars again."

Anaïs Nin

Printed in Great Britain
by Amazon